The Brave Little Tailor

retold by Stacey Sparks
illustrated by Catherine Kanner

Scott Foresman

Editorial Offices: Glenview, Illinois • New York, New York
Sales Offices: Reading, Massachusetts • Duluth, Georgia
Glenview, Illinois • Carrollton, Texas • Menlo Park, California

NARRATOR: Once there was a little tailor. He was very proud of himself.

TAILOR: I am such a fine tailor! I am such a clever fellow! I am—SO HUNGRY! I have been sewing all day. I need something to eat, but all I have is a dry piece of toast. How boring!

VOICE OUTSIDE: Jam for sale. Good jam!

NARRATOR: The tailor bought some jam for his toast. He ate a few bites. Then he put down the toast and went back to work.

NARRATOR: While the little tailor was sewing, some flies came in the open window. They landed on the sweet, sticky jam.

FLIES: Buzz! Buzz!

NARRATOR: When the tailor picked up his toast to finish it, he saw seven flies stuck to the jam.

TAILOR: Yuck! Flies! Well, I must be brave! I will have to get rid of them!

NARRATOR: The tailor threw the toast—and the flies—out the window. Then he was even more proud of himself than before. He wanted the world to know about the amazing thing he had done. So he made a belt to tell the tale.

5

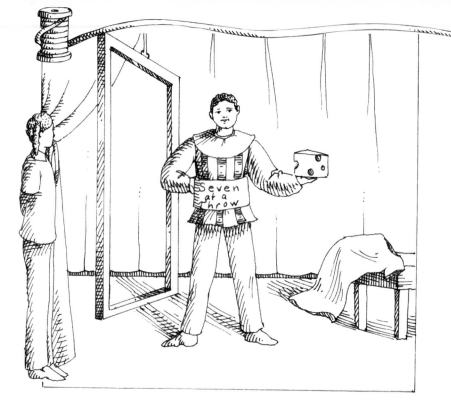

TAILOR: I just got rid of seven monsters with one throw. I was not born to stay at home and be a tailor! Out into the world I must go! I will fight other monsters. Maybe I will marry a princess. But first, I will get a handy chunk of cheese to take on my trip. Just in case I get hungry!

NARRATOR: The tailor set off down the street. People looked at his belt. They were puzzled.

WOMAN 1: Did you see his belt?

MAN 1: "Seven at a throw!" Sounds scary!

WOMAN 2: But what does it mean?

MAN 2: Who threw? Seven what?
Threw where?

TAILOR: I threw seven monsters out the
window!

WOMAN 1: Monsters?

TAILOR: Big, hairy, scary, buzzing, horrible
monsters with wings!

NARRATOR: The tailor kept walking. Soon he came to the woods. There he found a poor little blackbird. It was stuck in a shrub. The tailor rescued the bird. Then he put it in his sack along with the cheese. He walked a little farther and met a giant.

GIANT: Hi! You're little. I'm big.

TAILOR: I bet you are very smart too.

GIANT: How did you know?

TAILOR: I could just tell. Can you tell that I am very strong?

GIANT: You? Strong? Ha, ha! You make me laugh!

TAILOR: Just look at my belt. "Seven at a throw" means I am strong.

GIANT: Really! Let's see who is stronger.

NARRATOR: So the giant picked up a rock. He squeezed it so hard that water came out. The tailor just smiled and took out his cheese.

TAILOR: I will squeeze milk out of my rock!

NARRATOR: Then he squeezed the cheese until milk came out!

TAILOR: I win!

GIANT: Let's have another contest! You boast that you can throw! So let's have a throwing contest.

NARRATOR: The giant threw a rock way up high. It took a long, long time to come down.

GIANT: Wow!

NARRATOR: Too bad it almost landed on his head.

TAILOR: My turn, big fellow!

NARRATOR: The tailor took the bird out of his sack. He pretended it was a rock and threw it up into the air. The bird flew away.

NARRATOR: Time passed. The tailor fell asleep. The giant kept looking up.

GIANT: It has to come down soon! You cannot be that strong, little tailor. No one can throw a rock so high that it never comes down! That's impossible!

NARRATOR: Just then, the king and some of his helpers passed by. When they saw the giant, they froze. For months, this giant had been stomping around the kingdom and scaring everyone.

GIANT: Boo hoo! Don't hurt me!

KING: Are you afraid of us, Giant?

GIANT: I thought little people like you were weak. But if this little tailor is stronger than I am, maybe you are too.

KING: What little tailor?

NARRATOR: The brave little tailor woke up.

TAILOR: Did someone say my name?

GIANT: Help! I am running away. Far away!

KING AND HELPERS: Look at his belt. "Seven at a throw!" Does that mean seven giants?

TAILOR: No, it means seven buzzing monsters.

KING: Tailor, you have rid my kingdom of a fearsome giant. How can I thank you?

TAILOR: Well, I always thought it would be nice to marry a princess!

13

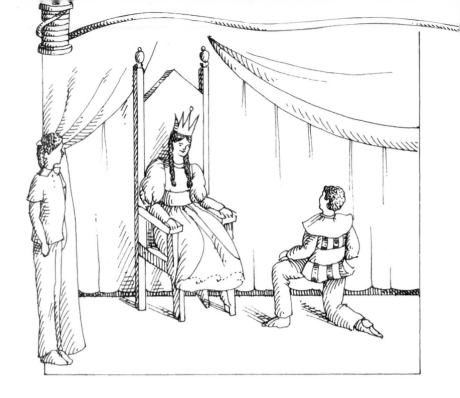

NARRATOR: So the king took the tailor home to meet his daughter.

PRINCESS: Thank you for getting rid of the giant. I am so scared of giants! I am also afraid of toads, barking dogs, and big, strong princes. You are not any of these things. Maybe I will marry you.

TAILOR: I am just a little tailor.

PRINCESS: But what about the seven monsters you got rid of?

TAILOR: Can you keep a secret?

PRINCESS: Absolutely!

TAILOR: They were not very big monsters.

PRINCESS: No?

TAILOR: In fact, they were quite little.

PRINCESS: How little?

TAILOR: They were about the size of a fly.

PRINCESS: Ha, ha!

TAILOR: In fact, they were flies.

NARRATOR: And so the princess married the little tailor. They had a splendid wedding. It was just like a fairy tale!